I0517372

Five Ghost Stories

DENNIS CALLACI

BAMBOO
DART
PRESS

LOS ANGELES † NEW YORK † LONDON † SYDNEY

Five Ghost Stories by Dennis Callaci

ISBN: 978-1-947240-05-6

eISBN: 978-1-947240-06-3

Copyright © 2021 Dennis Callaci. All rights reserved.

First Printing 2021

A round on me to all of our ghosts

Endless appreciation to Sara Adkisson and Simon Joyner for their help in editing and being a second and third pair of eyes on these stories.

cover art Dennis Callaci, layout Mark Givens

For information:

Bamboo Dart Press

chapbooks@bamboodartpress.com

Curated and operated by Dennis Callaci and Mark Givens

Bamboo Dart Press 003

www.pelekinesis.com

www.bamboodartpress.com

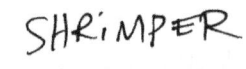

www.shrimperrecords.com

Contents

Model Home

We lost the directions, maybe in the rush to open the thing? We were so hungry to get started that we went in blind with only our logic and experience. We had pieced together so many models previously, that instead of waiting for some solution next weekend at that hobby store, we decided to work in the dark. This was Dracula's Castle. We had saved up two months of allowances between us after slobbering up the shop window where a prefab version was on display along with other models by the same company—World War II fighter planes, Big Ben, other non-fiction varieties. Nah, not for us, we needed escape, I thought. At last, we feverishly sat with the plastic overwrap of the box discarded between us, guide free.

The set came with Dracula, Frankenstein and The Wolf Man, a trio of classic Universal monsters built to semi-resemble Bela and Chaney, though far enough from their facial features that there would be no cease and desist lawsuits. I understood why the Creature from the Black Lagoon wasn't present, and somewhat the absence of the Invisible Man, but The Mummy was as good a fit as The Wolf Man. The castle seemed like a place that he would reside more so than Larry Talbot or Larry Talbot transformed with teeth. No Mummy. We would have to rectify that by building one up. Check the size of those green army figures, maybe shave one up with my pocket knife. Bulk the figure up with glue before whittling again and from there, paint and age it.

We wanted to tend to the monsters first. Snap, snap, snap there is Dracula, and then again and again until the monsters are unbound from their bondage. I had shown my younger brother how to sand off the nubs left by the plastic teeth of the punch-out. He is at it, gently building the nodule on Frankenstein's head, arms and feet away. This one, it came painted with decals, but of late, we had been using our model paints to add finer details, mend up any mass-produced blemishes or colors that needed to be addressed. I am the king of this here model, and he knows it. He is little brothering. Surrendering to me his money and attention, as well, when I can direct it my way. He finishes with his work on the creatures and goes back to being transfixed by the full-color cardboard box.

This model won't be that hard to build. It is a snap-together set, manufactured for kids without dads. We move to laying out the castle. I gather up the pieces for the varying sections which are for the most part locked together in sheets save for a few of the larger constructs. He pushes down on the milk-bone teeth to get the pieces free from the frames. Locking them together, building the spire of the tower. It looks cool, but I don't recall seeing spires on Dracula's castle.

The entirety of the piece has a main floor where the creatures are supposed to live. It is an open set with us facing the missing wall. There is a staircase coming down from a second story that we cannot peer into. Hollowed out, enclosed plastic. On the box, this is where the Wolf Man howls, on the steps. Once we have the parlor somewhat put together, my brother tries to get the figure in the exact location as it appears on the box. On the cover in full-color, there are sixteen steps, with our model there are only thirteen. He is having a difficult time with this.

"I don't care, it can go on step five or eleven, it doesn't matter to me," I tell him. He *plunk plunk plunks* the Werewolf's heavy heels down the steps.

"The werewolf that came with the set is not a toy, it's part of the model," I say reaching to get the werewolf out of his hand.

"It is not a werewolf, it is the Wolf Man," he says matching my tenor.

"Can't you see, I am working on the most difficult part? Can I get some quiet, please?" This sentiment comes from my mom, but here I was saying it to him now in the same timbre and tone that she would employ when telling one or the other of us to keep it down.

In my mind, I see a moat. There is not a moat and there is no drawbridge but I am working up a drawbridge with toothpicks, glue and line from Mom's sewing kit. I choose the yellow threading, a regal color. My creation is drying, propped up by a couple of plastic-coated decks of playing cards of the non-stick variety. There is so much that they leave out of these models, the blanks you have to fill in with your imagination or your bird-nest gathering abilities in a house without much excess to pull from.

I once used up nearly an entire roll of tinfoil for a moon landing. It wasn't until I was done that I panicked. *Mom is going to kill me.* I pulled the least rumpled blanket of the aluminum up from the runoff of the two astronauts (formerly army men) and rewrapped it around the cardboard roll. I hid the model for weeks from mom even after seeing her use the last of the recycled lunar terrain cover for our leftover meatloaf. She didn't take much interest. A few weeks out, I thought, she wouldn't even recognize the material as aluminum. Kids. Flawed logic in the place of what was actually indifference. Half of the fun of making these models was filling in the empty space, correcting the plot holes, making the piece your own. We scurried and plotted, brother and I, to bring our treasure home. Under our care, we dusted and oversaw our collection, shared them with friends, based stories around them.

The lunar landing, for instance, got play in the eves after dusk. The soundtrack to *2001* (left with a number of other records by our Pop) playing while we used flashlights to imagine ourselves as encased astronauts popping in to our ship for a snack, some clay form of popcorn and space age Tang. After a minor break, our plastic men went back to work planting flags. The reflected light, stars on our ceilings, our bunk beds, the wooden shutters on the windows. It wouldn't be until years later that we would see *2001* and then jigsaw our Wendy Carlos memories into the Kubrick scenery.

Blue Danube, Atmospheres, Lux Aeterna—those were imagined names of planets to us then, each with its own history, customs, different strains of alien breeds. They were vivid to me as I entranced my brother with off-the-cuff stories at bedtime. My favorite was a tribe of amoeba shape-shifting sentients I had called "The Wound." At this late date, I still cannot see or imagine their actual physical form. I described it as gelatinous and simplified it for him as a bean bag, a galaxy of little amorphous elves fitting into anything. They could be carbon or water, minute shale stone, sediment. My description was not enough to build a vision upon for either of us. The astronauts were retired soon and we started scavenging from their little world for our next build.

Big brother giving his little brother the last easy piece to snap in. Mom would be proud of me. I repositioned the Werewolf after getting Dracula to the foreground (it is his castle, after all) and Frankenstein to the far left of the staircase to balance the picture out. My brother starts crying.

"What's wrong?" He looks at me with his lower lip trembling.

"It's not like on the box, it needs to be like on the box." It is late, we had already pretended to be in bed. "I'm going to tell Mom." His voice desperate as it rises an octave, "I'm going to tell Mom." I grab him by both his arms and shake him.

"Don't you even dare. I will never play with you again if you do."

He breaks out, full sob, and crawls into his bed. I keep working, ignore him as his sobs turn to snores. He has been asleep at least an hour before I finish fine-tuning the thing. It is hard to tell time in the dark without a clock in your room.

In the morning, I awake to my brother sitting before the model again as though it were a pulpit of possibility. We were barely done with our last snap, but we had plans for the work that still needed to be done. We race into the bathroom, grab some cotton balls to turn into webbing. The castle will create a hunger for strobe and black lights, for a huge cardboard slab backdrop and soundtracks from our crappy stereo. This castle is somewhere to go, where the creatures are always home.

Michael's

The stench of the place announced itself before you even made it through the front door. That old Michael's Market where neither the air conditioning nor the soapy bleach ambience could push away the acrid breath of that meat corner. My mother casually strolled past the case with its Saran-wrapped stacks of polystyrene bottoms sandwiching pink, worm meal. I was at her side, a mutant cartoon child—*Fangoria* magazine, *Re-Animator* imagining. *Motel Hell, Texas Chainsaw* spawning that ground chuck. Farmers in Texas and Wisconsin were the very thing that nightmares were made of.

At seven years old, my father and I were watching horror movies in his apartment on the weekend. My friends didn't believe me, accused me of lying, acting badass. They could only imagine the thrill of those planted cut throats, fleshy wet meat masks. None of those films were as scary as the veined cuts, lifeless legs captured here. Or maybe this was scarier because of them, but any which way I absolutely abhorred this. Being here with mom who insisted that I not wander off in the market. In the meat section. Oh, to wander off.

Grocery shopping was something she and I did together, usually on weekday nights after dinner. *Why can't you save it for the week-end when I am with dad.* I'd tiny finger through the grates of the cart on the opposing side of the display cases, my green turtleneck collar pulled up over my nose as my mom put her cuts in the upper carriage of the thing. I'd be looking at the canned bean dip, generic tortilla chips through the plastic window of an undyed bag, anything to get the thought of them disjointed pieces floating in brine out of my mind, the smell out of my nose. Always wear a turtleneck when you go to the grocery store even if it's dirty, caked with dried pea soup, I reminded myself. Dig hurriedly through the hamper, get that thing on quick while she has keys in hand impatiently waiting so she can cross her list to get home and relax after another long day. As much as I hated Michael's, sometimes, she'd let me throw in a six pack of RC Cola for the weekend.

Another Monday. Another pick up. Another drop off. My aunt would finish her shift babysitting me and my cousin, Randy. Mom's second shift of the day was pinched between her day job and her four-hour smoke break. I was slung along—laundry run, gas station fill-up, a drop off for some so-and-so or something. I was inserted between all of those tasks.

Sure, there were bumps, bruises, but it was a good life for mom and me. Bad days in elementary school turned around on a dime by small things. My allowance unlocked bubble gum, comic books, cap guns and other deep-sixed childhood ephemera. I walked two blocks from our door to La Bodega where Lemonheads, Boston Baked Beans and Jerky were mine for the two bills in hand. I escaped into the glow of the TV or the spine of science fiction books from the library. I didn't want for anything. Well, almost anything.

My mom, I loved how she smelled when she walked through the door. *So long, aunt Florence and your idiot son. Mom is here now, I can smell it.* Florence rushed to trunk some bags or boxes of whatever it was she loaded and unloaded with every visit in a flurry to get out of our house. A bulldozer on a reverse escalator, she walked like a T-Rex in slicked-up heels. *Don't take your time, Flo. Please, leave as soon as you can.* I moved my lips through the screen door watching. Randy hopped onto the front seat. I hated his chubby little calves, his sailor shorts. *Goodbye fuckers*, I mouthed, not voicing it. *Fuckers*, thank you *Motel Hell*.

My mom, some kind of disciple of Saint Nick. How else could she know that Michael's was the perfect penance for her little boy? Atonement for conjuring a gruesome murder scene of her sister and her nephew. Was I mouthing the words, just under my breath maybe as I cursed the two of them? How she knew my curses and thoughts was beyond me. Was there a mirror reflecting back the frontside of me? Some device constantly recording these thoughts and actions? *Off to the torture garden with you.*

Michael's Market, up the aisle with canned jalapenos, olives, pickles, and then just a few steps until we got to the pickled pigs' feet. In my mind, this delicacy was housed in polycarbonate jars so that were one to fall, it would not shatter and disturb the shoppers with the hazmat police, the oxygen tanks falling down from the drop ceiling. Those poor sows, clumping around on clotted stumps of scarred straw sealant, I thought. The shoppers or the footless pigs? Good question, I think back. Did she even lift the jar off of the shelf? Did she call attention to it? I don't think so. On the metal shelves, zero-gravity jars of their little feet rested like Barbie & Ken accessories. Into the cart some jarred dill relish was placed.

We lived in the low-rent, so these leaps of my imagination were minor compared to where they would go as I got older and was able to take in the torture that the well-heeled enjoyed. It was not enough for them to see the bodies and the parts pickled, plastic-wrapped or frozen. No, for their impeccably curated and finely-lit museums they added the bonus attraction of actual living beings in bondage, killed on order, your choosing! Those rubber-banded lobsters, huddled one on top of the other unaware of the darker landings that awaited them.

This, a true moment of rejoice for the sadistic-leaning pescatar-ians, those choosing to take the odd soul home to endure further suffering before a good boiling. As if that were not enough, the carcass shoved through their inhuman bodies, excreted into a ba-sin of tubes and plumbing into a huge water treatment facility where they would mingle with bile, vomit and insects drowned with but a single ply of toilet paper. What kind of end is this? Holy shit, Joe Goebbels must have feasted on lobster nightly knowing this chain of events, the before and aftering. I had an aversion to lobster long before seeing them tanked, gagged and sold in the market. Cockroaches of the sea, my Mom called them. *When I am rich, I am going to eat the cockroach of the sea*, I'd singsong joyously trying for hours to get her to crack even the smallest of a smile. I won a couple of times, minor cracks in cement, tiny dents for me to digest.

I've spent my adult life as a vegetarian, so you would think that my life would be fairly free from these side wanderings that tripped me up as a youth. You don't see death daily if you don't want to. After all, it is fairly easy to avoid as the markers are ex-clamation-pointed. Don't stop for a sip of water at the slaughter-house off of the Grapevine. Don't get a job with animal control or become a cop. When you are at a hospital, keep your eyes to yourself, and should it be someone you love, and they are taking in their last breath, you won't have to stay with the body for very long. In fact, it will still be warm when you leave the room and won't yet resemble a carcass.

So, why is it, as one who owns no animals, that I am caring for so many dead or dying of their species? The black cat splayed out on my lawn. Her tiny head held on by a tendon after a Chupacabra of a mangy coyote has ripped the poor girl apart. Me, awkwardly shoveling the thing into a thirty-two gallon black trash bag while the eldrely neighbor jogs by. The huge raccoon covered in ants at the backdoor which I nearly squashed into upon returning from a vacation as I made my way to the bins with month-old news-paper. *How long were you there? You and I again, dead friend, shovels and bags.* The poisoned rat on Easter morning, panting cross-eyed in the shrubs. *Goddamn it, did it ingest enough to take itself out? Do I need to brick-smash the sad thing?*

Those three deaths all happened within a year of one another. Maybe this is the every day. Maybe you go through the same. A reprieve here or there but the work never ends. By the time you get rid of that haunted smell and the memory of it all starts to lose its sharpness, it is replaced by another in the series. I hope not, but I also hope for myself, that I am not alone in this.

If you ever happen to be in my company, and there are carcasses of any kind around, let this serve as a warning. They flock to me, the undertaker for the poverty-stricken and empty-pocketed animal set. They know that I will act quickly, not panic. They must have alerted the animal kingdom in some kind of Aquaman tenor that is unheard by humanity, for it is not simply this triptych in that one year. I am souping dead opossums out of the neighbor's pool, tending to the dead bird in the middle of the park that the kids are rock stick fiddling with. If I am not called, I will come nevertheless, dispatched from my makeshift phonebooth of the mind with bag in hand. It is not something I enjoy, nor want to do, but I will do it. Does a doctor want to operate? Does the jury want to deliberate? No, but we all do what we must, every day.

The Cemetery of Calendar Days

Be careful tonight. My wife cupped my ears with her hands, a kiss on the way out the door. There had been seven in the last month in my line including two colleagues I was close to. Down the steps, "Be careful honey, I love you." I took her car tonight with three-quarters of a tank, I didn't want to risk any stop this evening that I needn't make. An oldie flashes out with ignition from the stereo, *Too Real by* Fontaines D.C.

The two of us worked hard to keep a sense of normalcy not only for our family, but the neighborhood, as well. Ann checking on the elderly, bringing dinner to at least a half-dozen families nightly. I would attempt emergency electric work that was beyond me, fixing up fallen siding to the best of my abilities. It wasn't like before. You couldn't always get a plumber or even a physician to respond in a timely manner. Hell, we had both been educated at some of the finer schools in the nation, knew about history, could easily draw parallels to this moment in time. The year zero reset, the surrendering of day-to-day. With all of the pillars of not only our lives, but everyone's in various states of decay, I felt more alive now than I had in decades. There was a new sensitivity and soft-ness in nearly all of my relationships. It stayed there most days, but would inch toward rawness and exasperation on the worst of them.

Before that spring a few years back, we had options, paths, room to play around the edges of near anything. Now the penned-up lines were rigid. The terms of what should and shouldn't be said. The current state brought the stumbling to light, humanity's attempts to stem the prehistoric tragedies of successive generations. Pompeii's ashen couples holding onto one another, Hitler's death caves where strangers together prayed, and those that were similar to this—the plagues, the outbreaks. This new blood-flow fed their memory and brought them to me, to those of us listening, in the round.

- = - = - = - = - = - = - = - = -

A wife in midtown kneels inches from her husband's face, repeating his name over and over again. His eyes are taking it in, thighs on the edge of the bed with his boots to the ground. He is conscious, and the panic between the two of them is palpable. "Honey, are you alright?" her voice rising. He is conscious, it is clear by his movement, his panic, but he can say nothing.

- = - = - = - = - = - = - = - = -

Ann is asleep with our youngest's favored on her chest. A kiss for each of our daughters after taking off and tending to all of my work-related things. There is a note on the counter from her, jotted down. Though she rarely sleeps anymore, she wanted to be sure I got these messages in the event she had fallen asleep before

I got home. Two calls, the meat of them written down. Both work related. I had dealt with one tonight, the other would have to wait until I caught sleep and awoke at dusk. That crew was off now, anyway.

It was another long shift of patrolling but mainly without incident. A break in the Adams' fence that I got the squad on. I couldn't tell who, if any, might have made it through in the time it'd been breached. No new picks-ups, no new discoveries. "Daniel?" Ann calls for me. It's into her arms and a coin toss for sleep. Maybe a brief snooze for the two of us before sunrise when the kids will be needing her attention.

⌐ ＝ ⌐ ＝ ⌐ ＝ ⌐ ＝ ⌐ ＝ ⌐ ＝ ⌐ ＝ ⌐ ＝ ⌐

The pay was good, but the dividends in corporate stock and bonuses were what made her position at RenTech palatable. Sure, there were upsetting sets of red tape and waste coupled with questionable practices but that was rampant everywhere. The church, the Stable Bureau, the civil servitude branches of altruists and fair-to-near-mint Samaritans all had touches of that as well. Your citrus trees don't turn out blemished fruit? This was, after all, a service that was considered section A1. She had the lanyard in her car with the laminated IDs and every security passcode on site memorized. The new regime was not stacked with the most creative of think tanks. Redundancy and banality was the track on which that train would run. A1. Warp speed. Terms created millennia ago that still managed to stay in the vernacular of those who seldom read.

Dallas oversaw the team that invented the Renread machine. A scientific and technological breakthrough that brought all languages, even dead ones, under one umbrella. The Renread had its scientific brethren; the cochlear implant, Irisight, Scentanol, all which treated senses that had become faint or latent. Dallas not only headed the development team, but in her newfound role was considered an Edison, Franklin or Jobs. Like them, she took credit for that which was not hers and appreciated the conversation that placed so much at her feet for the sake of shorthand ease.

The Renread had been in use for over eight years and had become a necessity for travelers and tourists as a means to quickly translate any language from their thoughts to the local tongue. The initial versions were clunky. A device worn outward on the body for those who could read. A quick one-day outpatient surgery required. A magnetized port was installed just above the dura of the cranium. The 1.0 to 2.5 out-of-reach for the less wealthy or surgically averse. That had changed just over a year ago. A simple prick as quick as an ear piercing performed in any hub station, allowing for a lifetime of service to the Renread.

RenTech's Renread 122 was a much simpler device that no longer needed the bulky screen which had made tourists sitting ducks for scams and muggings. The latest version allowed for the user to speak in the owner's selected language and was utilized in manners previously unimagined. It became a go-to shower gift for expectant parents, allowing them to understand their newborn's requests. A surgery allowing the device to be used on pets had a waiting list of over six months but was still prototypes away. The future was clear. Around the bend there would be disposable versions at toy stores for kids to attach sticky-handed onto, butterflies, popascules, worms and recoravamps. Attach it to anything you can capture or get your arms around to hear its secret inner life speaking.

The market share and the spread of RenTech then, there was no stopping them. The new formats would provide a lift, but not large enough to float the once dominant company much longer. The overhead nut and thousands of employees were borrowing against the company's liquid future. Dallas had been bolting the door, working against time just months after the silence virus, Dysarthria Simplex. She was trying to find a way for those who had lost the ability to communicate with their loved ones. Not just in hopes of turning around the company and her stock portfolio but for her own well being and that of those she loved. For now she had succumbed. She knew her attempt to be secretive about her condition wouldn't last, she could only dodge phone calls and avatar meetings for so long.

～ = ～ = ～ = ～ = ～ = ～ = ～ = ～

The run-off channels had been problematic as we got into the second summer. The inch-deep of trickling was never going to dissuade an on-foot interloper. Blocking off an exit or entry to a four-foot linked channel ravine wasn't going to do anything. These became main patrols even after laying down nail-to-heaven carpeting three yards apart in the drains. Those breaking in weren't animals, they had methods and means. The city managers and council couldn't agree on how serious a threat any of this was which served as a perfect device of divide. The gods would be so impressed at what a quick end this organism that had evolved to conquer all other living beings was moving to meet its extinction. After all of the quakes and hurricanes and flooding, this would be our mass graveside landing. What were we now, a generation, maybe two from the last of our kind? That truism still rings, leave them to their own devices and they will even knot their own noose for you.

Here, though, we weren't through. Andrew's optimism married to his distrust of humanity was difficult for even him to carry. He had lost a son to this even after taking every precaution. Once Lucas fell ill, they had used every remedy on hand but nothing pulled him through. His child was one of the anomalies that scared the hell out of anyone that had read the scroll of the story, or even just heard it brought up as a statistic. No underlying symptoms, a perfectly healthy six-year-old child, dead within three months after that first diagnosis.

His wife was against him staying on the force but she couldn't argue with his reasoning. Besides, what else were they supposed to do? Move to another municipality where the same troubles were in play, where they knew no one? The community had been as supportive and loving as you would hope given these circumstances. As the months wore on, they had discussed moving. It was getting harder to live with all of those eyes upon them. He heard another just the other day outside of The Blue Star. "That's the guy whose son died of the Silence." He was out for a bite on his lunch break, alone with his paper. With what strength remained, he kept a chin up. It was easier to pretend he couldn't hear them as they flashed weak smiles and turned away. *What kind of protection can he offer us if he couldn't even keep his kid safe,* he hears in the unsaid.

"So, we move somewhere else and introduce ourselves to the new neighbors, how is that going to be? Hi, we're The Redman's. You might recognize us from that headline about our child having died from Silence." He couldn't believe he was saying this. Rae ran out of the room in tears at the drop of it. It left the two of them paralyzed with no moves any which way.

Dead from the Silence. It was a deafening moan and writhing until the morphine came. No one should ever have to hear such things, not from their dearest. You feel like dying every day. I can't breathe easy no more when every breath gets me further from my baby. My baby, under my care, underground. I'm feeling fine, for maybe two hours, and then a memory. One of them with Silence wandering the see-through fencing, taunting me. You don't know about Lucas. You can't see through me, you sonofabitch. Right now, I haven't the strength to prevent the torching of the entirety of this planet. For if it would take all of you to end all of this suffering, that would be reason enough to stand with arms behind my back, sideline lit by the flames of it.

"Another one, quick, side-flash to the left!›› The high-power lamplights flash on to track the scattering just outside of the perimeter of the fence. The lights were employed only after there was enough security on hand to safely beat back any ambushes lying in wait. Things had changed recently with the deaths of a veteran and his partner, a new cadet. Both were found beaten to death in front of their patrol car with the engine running, hi-beams looming out just over their bodies. The disease starts as a loss of language but over a prolonged period and without the base treatment breakthroughs prescribed to the afflicted, further senses declined. There had been a plethora of cases involving vision and hearing loss, some were even saying that the other senses (taste and smell in some samplings) as well as skin diseases were tied to the virus. Patrolling was made easier working against the afflicted in these technologically dependent times. Utilizing their intact senses was tool one in any CS Squadron and didn't rely on forever-changing tech knowledge.

The CS needed to be on hand fairly quickly behind patrol to mend any breaches that had occurred at hot spots. Rebar, concrete, chain link, rabbit proofing. "If those freaks wouldn't have started that separatist movement, we wouldn't have this problem." Andrew spits. At first a group of three neighbors living in the same stretch of a neighborhood refused treatment and saw their new malady as an act of god, of being touched. Over the ensuing months, neighbors reported break-ins at night, savagery that was soon linked to the stricken trio when a wife of one of them filed a police report. On a news broadcast she said the criminal wasn't even recognizable to her as her dear husband.

Soon, neighbors moved out the vicinity and, in time, citizen vigilantes escorted the true believers to the boondocks off of south Vineyard in the lower reaches of Rancho Cucamonga. "Find your kind," they were told as they were curb-kicked, kissed goodbye by their loved ones. What began on the down-low like skid row drop offs soon became a city ordinance as security fencing went up around the northern regions. "We are locking ourselves tight, not blocking anyone's right to move freely," became a favored rallying cry.

The scouts had found no one on foot within the ten-mile radius of whirring reds and bloodhounds over the last two or so hours. The breach had been mended and the two of them would be back at the station shortly to fill out a report with the details. There were no visible losses tonight, but it hardly mattered. They'd pushed beyond the point of anything resembling the past long ago.

- = - = - = - = - = - = - = - = - = - = -

"The willful transability, lack of respect for humanity..." one Sunday talk show commentator to another. "We have seen this in cities all across our country and to a far lesser extent globally where the medical cocktail and rush for a vaccine is a priority for most world leaders and its citizenry." It was true. What started as a cult slid into the mainstream vernacular, equating wild rumors with science and fact. Because the transmission of the Silence was yet to be fully understood, some didn't fear the possibility of infection at this late date. They assumed that if they hadn't gotten it yet, it would not get to them. Others, hiding behind curtains, communicating via the breathing space in their electric firewalls worried themselves to sleep.

Each passing day hardened opinions. The middle stretched to a breaking point. Soon, it would snap and there would no longer be an arch between sides, just two stubby ends.

Dallas took her daily doses and could do all but speak now, utilizing pads of paper and computer screens. She spent her evenings on self-prescribed experimental trials for one. Appearing as "Ms. Burling" in her journals should they be confiscated. It wasn't illegal to do such but it was frowned upon by her peers to experiment on oneself. Ethics? Philosophical debate? Late night dead ends over drinks? There was no longer time for that. This was the new Dallas, the new paradigm. She was not, in fact, a mad scientist. This was moving at a faster clip than sci-fi pulp. She was feverish, getting near to something revelatory, but calling it a breakthrough would be far too sanguine for her analytical mind. A mind that was still in full bloom as other faculties were being evicted.

- = - = - = - = - = - = - =

In time, large swaths of homes in the upscale neighborhoods started to resemble those of their working class cousins. Wrought fences of iron, barred windows and public places abandoned now that they were without the shield of security. The self-imposed lockdown and social divisions were no longer theoretical. Shops were still open. Main street still had parking meters, but no one minded them anymore, not the city or the residents. The old downtown, with its quaint wooden storefront signs and composite boardwalk wasn't as spooky now as it was a year ago. Residents had turned a blind eye to its cosmetic failings. The jewel of the community now resembled an old friend that had taken a southbound turn in your absence. Tumbleweeds blew from the Santa Ana winds.

Today, it retained hints of what it once was. There were lights on in the shops, folks walked the streets with knotted plastic bags with styrofoam leftovers, a child's knee scrape being tended to beneath an entryway alcove. I pulled up in the squad car. Even when off-duty, the county had deemed that CS employees should always drive them as an added veneer of security.

I used to make appointments but there wasn't a need for that now. My barber, George, welcomed me with a great big smile, dapper as ever in his brown slacks and white button-up collar.

"Have a seat young man, I can see you are needing your regular trim." George and I had discussed the most tender and hilarious of things in his place. Well, he did most of the discussing, I mainly listened in this rented chair. We had been doing this for at least a few decades now. George asks about my family, whatever other small talk that is left for us to kick around. Maybe because there's simply not enough of that brand of talk anymore, exhausted of it and nearly done with his job, he moves on. He gently pushes down the back of my neck to finish.

"Daniel, what are you doing about that mess out there?" I lift up my head, he turns off the clippers, dusts me and spins the chair around to the mirror to see.

"Looks good, thank you, George." I pause for just a second and then before he can get a word in, "You read the scrolling update, you know what we're up against. *What do you mean, what am I do-ing?*" My job used to be a point of pride for me. I felt it when someone asked me what I did for a living, or even now, when I pulled into the station some mornings, unrushed.

"Doesn't look like much," he says even-toned. "I think that may-be you should all be treating this a bit more seriously."

The events of the last few years had changed everyone, not just those infected or *touched*. I wasn't the same agreeable guy that he'd known all of these years. We never had much to get heated up about. There was an unspoken respect, we would let the conversa-tion rest if we hit a touchy subject in the past.

"Well, basically I've become some kind of mall cop guarding property for the wealthy," I tell George, peeved.

"Ha, that is what you have been since you took that job, Big D!"

Fucking George.

"Well then, George, I am doing what I have always done about every mess. That's me, cleaning it up while you cut hair." I noticed this in other relationships of mine. This is how it always seems to start. Little seeds of dissension between family, friends, co-work-ers that we used to let pass. Nothing passes now without a thor-ough inspection.

Is it paranoia when the whispers start to come true? It is no longer a threat, it is upon us. I spent my time tamping down delu-sions and keeping my tight-buttoned worries under wraps. I know what it means when authority begins to admit to defeat, the nod to the notion that nothing much can be done. George undoes the collar of the apron after a more thorough dusting off of fallen hair. We try to end it on high, but there is a wire of tension standing, and I just leave it there with the kindest, "Thank you, George, see you next time," that I can muster.

- = - = - = - = - = - = - = - = - = -

She used to stand there, at the foot of the stage for presentations to shareholders. Sometimes a prop behind a speech by a Governor, hell, even the president. Those stages don't exist right now. If they did, what would she do anyhow? Power-point the odd failed experiments that had damaged her health in other ways? The last MRI was more bad news. More symptoms of the Silence increasing and encroaching.

Last week, she put in her leave. She had already cut off her daily communique with friends and colleagues months ago with no explanation. They were bright. Some of them had intimated their concern. *Dallas, haven't heard from you in a while, how is the project coming along?* When was the last time she had spoken? Nearly four months ago? She had told them that she was close and needed all of the time she could get to work from her annex. RenTech complied. They, too, were pushing all the chips on their table into her corner. There weren't many other options. She could imagine their discussions in her absence "...give her a few months, look at what she delivered before." That was what she had been hoping for even as she prepared for this possibility.

A lovely evening, a wonderful meal of curried lamb, black chana, raita, wine. Evening dew had blanketed all the patio furniture, she turned to her bedroom, the vial on the nightstand.

RenTech stocks dropped over forty percent with the first bullet of the news. Worse, word had gotten out from one of Dallas' colleagues after markets closed that day that the breakthrough drug that was nowhere near a reality. Trading would be furious in the AM. The CEO of the company asked a stone-faced board of directors, "Anyone have a plan as to how we stem this bleeding?" The VP, typically stoic, struck an emotional tone, "Johnette Dallas committed suicide last night. What does that indicate to all of you?" No one thought Sears-Roebuck would fail, nor Wal-Mart or Apple, but corporations were like people, they died as well, only in slow motion. The compounded issues tied to this news did not bode well for a company in free fall that had been hedging their bets on the pharmaceutical division.

＜ ＝ ＜ ＝ ＜ ＝ ＜ ＝ ＜ ＝ ＜ ＝ ＜ ＝ ＜ ＝ ＜

I snuck in pre-dawn, peeled off my clothes for a quick shower then pulled Ann's warm body next to me. It had been an uneventful shift, no break ins, no sightings. The two of us breathing, in different states of waking with the kids still sleeping. It was Sunday, wasn't it? That meant coffee in bed, kids skirting around us, an ease-up for the four of us. I turned to face Ann to jokingly throw her nickname in that awful TV jingle, but I found it difficult to mouth the words. I lay there for a while, tilting from my side to my back again. I knew this would be the last time we'd be like this, Ann and me. I wanted to simply stay there as long as I could.

"Are the kids awake? Daniel, are the kids awake?" She shook me to see if I had fallen asleep. I don't think she saw the tears welling in my eyes. "Daniel, honey, are you OK?" I couldn't say.

Discarded Ghost Stories

The wind had double-backed and with a flick of its forefinger, plucked the oversized straw hat from his crown and to the roadside as he attempted to get out of his truck on the soft shoulder of the road. It was a hundred-and-three and nearly five PM. He should already be on the route back home, but for this. He had grown up watching his father doing these same sorts of routines to mostly stellar effect—a buck for someone short at the grocers, a ride for a hitchhiker, a peer under the hood of a coughing car. His father's actions carried the weight of omnipotence, animation delivered to us from above, compelling us to take the high moral ground, even in times of duress or shortness. The two of them never talked about these actions after the act, there was no need. Usually, the attended with he and his father did that. Talked in these places that they didn't.

He pulled behind the Saturn with oxidized paint. It was late afternoon and he could see the abandoned tire change. Hell, he had a cell phone and AAA, this wasn't brain surgery. A small elderly woman with doors locked and windows cracked was on the drive side - some stuffed animals in the back windshield, but no other passengers. He wasn't an imposing man, but this world with its trust worn paper-thin doesn't always abide when a stranger inserts himself into someone's vulnerability. It's sometimes not worth that bother, much less the risk. The poor door-to-door census workers dealing with the tinfoil-capped and newspaper-windowed deserters of the factual world can attest to that. He inched up behind the Saturn, not wanting to pull too close behind the beached car or park in front and box it in. *Distance, stranger, distance.*

Who resides in that auto? What weaponry is at the ready? Gun in the glovebox? Knife up the sleeve? Why would he put himself in harm's way? He wasn't a cop, had no grand design to be Samaritan Sam. Decency for a fellow traveler - dignity and an S.O.S. delivery. He could remember vividly the time that a stranger picked up a tab for him at a restaurant. Who? Where? Why? What did it matter? It was kind. The two sandwiches that his sophomore Civics teacher packed - one for her and one for him - over lunch at the end of class, during lunch break when he had nowhere to go, and no lunch of his own that he could afford. There is sweetness and light all around, but it's just that, not concentrated, and not easily seen. This was on his mind and in his back pocket. His therapist called it a martyr's checkbook.

He saunters up slow, just past the side rearview so as to not give her a start had she not seen him pull up. He crouches down and into the slice of the window asks if she is okay, if she needs help. She speaks in Mandarin, maybe Cantonese. He shrugs his shoulders, speaks a bit of pigeon sign language, points back to her tire. He pulls out his phone and offers it to her. They are getting nowhere, the two of them.

Should he hang around, leave, alert the authorities? Sometimes you think you are helping someone out, but you're not. You are just another sheet of their unraveling. He could picture a number of scenarios at play, possible entry and exits to this story. Maybe the tire was the second thing gone wrong that day. Maybe she needed a rental space to land other weight and this isn't the place. *Don't insert yourself too quickly. Be on the lookout for rattlesnakes, always. Use words economically. Most importantly, look down at the ground when you speak.*

It had never unfolded like this with his dad. No one had ever been gunned or robbed or stabbed which he half-expected. His father had never shown a lack of resolve or inability to move- not this chessboard of cement, not this muted language he was in the thickets with. His phone, his car and this. None of it created any common ground from which to kindly exit.

She looked dead on. Minutes like hours, this paralysis of action started to make him nervous, owning a nervous energy of hers he thought he picked up. He pulled his hat from up against his calf where it had been pinned by the wind. He got in his truck, left her where she was, kindly doffed the rim of the now seated hat and waved with his right window down as he drove away. He could think of nothing else to do. The way home, he felt spent thinking about that poor old lady. Would she still be there come Monday? *What shouldn't I do? Right. You shouldn't do anything. Don't bother telling Marina about it, don't bring it up on Sunday over lunch with your brother and sister-in-law.* It was a dead end, but no one got hurt, and no one is,in fact, dead at the end.

Still, the memory haunted him into next week. He took the freeway to work, and though it was a Monday and traffic was never as bad as on Friday, he took those same side streets home, right on Baker just to see. *What? Mummified remains? The lady still sitting in the dust of her car waiting?* Our minds, our bodies, they have lives of their own. They impel us to do ridiculous things. Back in the house to put your hand lightly on the iron, is it off? They don't always work in tandem with one another.

The car was gone, he saw that her battered hubcap remained where the car had been. She must have gotten home okay, towed, who knows. Maybe a family member or friend came to the rescue. He pulled up and parked in her space. His keys were still dancing in the ignition as he closed his eyes. Maybe he nodded for a few minutes, maybe twenty. A rush of wind from a passing truck shook him awake. Hands on his thighs, stretching his legs beyond the brake and gas pedals, he checked the rearview and saw nothing behind him. He flipped down the turn signal as he pulled into his lane.

The Sundowner

I'm no longer who I was. I tried hard to remember who that had been for a good long while, couldn't quite reckon with it, but I know it's true. I don't feel the same. I cheer for different ball teams, don't care no more about gardening or the TV. I wonder if this is halfway to sundown. We never know where the middle or the end is. Cut short at twenty-two? Convalescing at a hundred and three? I've had both in my family. It didn't help me none to know that. I frequented the same restaurant three times a week for over a decade, then one day, just stopped. Stopped that white bag take-out, red tray solo company with the newspaper. I guess my subscription just ran out. My body was fulled-up as far as it could go and didn't want to visit the smell or the taste of Lily's anymore is all, I suppose. I think of it now only because I am trying to get to that place a day before some weighty change hits. Inch by inch, quietly happening right now, right under my nose. Waiting to take me back on some delivery date that I've got no tracking number for. You don't think about it before it arrives, even less once it's gone. In the thick of it though, that's where you get stuck.

There was a homeless dude, Abe, that used to sweep the sidewalk in front of the strip joint that I worked for. He swept all day. He would sweep the same cement cracks with the "disco sux" carved in the corner. Five minutes after finishing that sidewalk square, he'd be right back at the top to do it again. I don't know what it was he was sweeping at. It was a furious movement like brushing away a wasp. I asked him once, years in, what he was sweeping. He looked at me, one eye closed, faced scrunched up, sizing me up in a *you fucking with me* sorta stare. "I'm sweeping," he said, "Is there a problem with that?" He's years gone, no idea where he went off to, but I'm still here, door leaning, slapping flyers into stranger's hands as they duck under the awning for shade or shelter from rain depending on the day. Same thing. I didn't wonder where it was or when it was that he went until he was long gone and I reasoned I would never see him again.

I have landed nearer to him than I would care to be. I see it in the reflective glass on my walk home. That's still me, barely, mainly someone else. *What in the hell am I going to do with this old man?* We sit down in the studio apartment above Novotney's Transmission. I play cards with him, hands that can be played for one serving. Slap three cards on top of three. Try to salvage a play. Hope for an eight of hearts or diamonds but a three of clubs can lift on top of the two resting on the ace. This is something that I can still do.

I go to bed by nine most nights. I can't stand the nights no more. I've taken to rising between four and five. I can slide open the blinds then, slit the window to get some cold air on summer mornings. The shop doesn't start humming until seven AM. A few hours of just me and a breeze, some black coffee and poached eggs. I listen to the streets. Strange seeing the endless parade of junior high kids still walking to school. I see none in the neighborhood, but they appear like clockwork making their way to every school day.

I don't get upset about the noise or the assholes, how they speed. I listen for the vagrants laughing or screaming at one another, themselves. I understand better what they are howling about now.

When I was a teenager, I saved for things. I was a newspaper boy as soon as I was of age. I kept my grades. Now, the newspaper comes to me, but most days, I barely unwrap it from its plastic. It is dead after all, it's been put to sleep. I don't look old, at least not as old as I had imagined I would at this age. I haven't become one of them Jimmy's. Jimmy Randall was an asshole that lived on my street who was always blaming some kid or other for ruining his lawn or marigolds or sneaking up to that retaining wall that wrapped his porch and stealing his strawberries. I did do that once, but once was enough. Scared the hell out of me to imagine him coming out shotgun. Old Jimmy. How old was he then? Dead now for sure.

I was a bouncer, but one day they told me they were reworking everyone's job responsibilities. They moved me outside, papering. I didn't see no one else get reworked. I guess that day I just got old, my muscles must've appeared to have weakened to the point of no longer being of use in the building. I worked fewer hours at the same hourly rate. I can't complain. I have become a fixture, even got interviewed by the local news woman, Sandy Ames, once when the liquor store next door caught flame and burned down.

I'm opening another bag of bread, putting spread on it, laying it out on one of the same five plates. They're fine plates, lasted me a good long while. Ms. Carroll, I hear her steps above the stairway. Some are afraid to leave this life or maybe afraid of the afterlife. I'm not afraid of that. I told Ms. Carroll (she has the room across from mine) that I would check on her once a day if she would do the same for me in the event of forgetting. She laughed, hugged me. First hug I'd had in a while. "Of course, William, let's do that." I just want to be gone once I'm gone. I don't want to be hanging around some rental above a garage, scaring the hell out of someone who finds me where I lay. That's been all I've been worried about of late, and now I don't have to worry about nothing. The sky is darkening, beautiful, isn't it? I pour myself a small and look at it from indoors after being out in it. It's a minnow, a minnow in the ocean.

112 N. Harvard Ave. #65

Claremont, CA 91711

chapbooks@bamboodartpress.com

www.bamboodartpress.com

www.ingramcontent.com/pod-product-compliance
Lightning Source LLC
Chambersburg PA
CBHW080756120626
46557CB00006B/1295